The Cool Ghoul Mystery

A Fletcher Mystery

by Elizabeth Levy
Illustrated by Mordicai Gerstein

Aladdin

New York London Toronto Sydney Singapore

To the Stowe Gang

First Aladdin Paperbacks edition November 2003
Text copyright © 2003 by Elizabeth Levy
Illustrations copyright © 2003 by Mordicai Gerstein

ALADDIN PAPERBACKS
An imprint of Simon & Schuster Children's Publishing Division
1230 Avenue of the Americas, New York, NY 10020

Also available in a paperback edition from Aladdin Paperbacks.
Designed by Lisa Vega
The text of this book was set in ACaslon Regular.

Printed in the United States of America
10 9 8 7 6 5 4 3 2 1

Library of Congress Control Number 2003109399

ISBN 0-689-86160-5

Contents

One

It's Snow Use

"Fletcher, stop bouncing!" complained Jasper. He held on to my ear. It was the first snow of winter. Jasper is my best friend. He just happens to be a flea.

Fleas hate winter. Jasper burrowed deeper into my fur. I am a fat basset hound who usually doesn't like to move. But there's something about a big pile of snow that just makes me want to roll in it and lick it. Maybe because it looks like whipped cream. Now if only snow came salami flavored.

"Look at Fletcher," cried Gwen. "He looks like

the abominable snowman bounding through the snow." Gwen is my owner Jill's best friend. It's not like her to call me abominable anything. I cocked

THE ABOMINABLE SNOWMAN IS A CREATURE SOME BELIEVE INHABITS REMOTE SNOWY REGIONS.

my head at her.

"It's okay, boy," said Jill, shaking the snow from on top of my head. "She just means that you look like a creature from a double feature."

Jill laughed. She threw a snowball at Gwen. They both giggled. It's hard not to giggle in the snow.

I bounded through the snow over to them. Jasper held on for dear life.

"I've never seen Fletcher move like that," shouted Jill. "Mom, come look at Fletcher."

Jill's mother stopped the snowblower that she was using on the driveway.

"Hi, Fletcher!" she shouted. I changed direction. My legs are short, and in order to move through snow, I've got to jump. I like looking back and seeing the tracks my four paws leave in the deep snow.

"Mom, we should take Fletcher on our winter vacation," yelled Jill.

Jill's mother smiled, but she shook her head no. "I already made a reservation for him at Paws Inn."

"What's Paws Inn?" asked Jasper.

"I think it's a hotel for dogs," I explained. "I like a good pause. It's kind of like a nap."

"I know about those places that take dogs when

their owners go on vacation," said Jasper. "They give flea baths. They hate fleas. We can't go there."

I hadn't thought about Jasper. Fleas are very tiny. Jasper, although a

fine flea, is just one-sixteenth of an inch long.
He does not have wings, but he does have
three pairs of legs that are great for jumping. However, when you're that
tiny, even if you're a great
jumper, you can't go far.

1/16"

A FLEA
JUMPING
ACTUAL
SIZE.

Most dogs hate fleas, but Jasper and I made a
deal a long time ago. He keeps other fleas off me.
He's become family. I couldn't have him die in a
flea bath in a strange hotel. I wondered how I could
get Gwen and Jill to take us with them on vacation.

I wagged my tail. That usually works with
humans. I gave Jill's mother my best grin.

"Look, Mom," said Jill. "Fletcher really wants to
come with us."

I just love that girl. I wagged my tail even faster.
Every time I wagged my stumpy little tail, the
snow tickled my butt. I guess that's something that

humans don't have to worry about in the snow, but it made me grin even wider.

"He really wants to come," said Gwen, seeing my big smile.

"Come on, Mom," said Jill. "We've never taken Fletcher on vacation. And we could save money if we took him."

"Please," begged Gwen. "You're being wonderful taking me, but it won't seem like a real vacation without Fletcher."

"Well, all right," said Jill's mother. "I'll call the lodge and see if they take pets."

We went into the house. Gwen and Jill had to take off their parkas and snowboots, but all I had to do was shake.

"Hey, watch it!" cried Jasper as he went flying through the air. He just barely held on to the tip of my tail as I shook the snow off myself in the front hall.

Jill's mother went to the phone. She dialed a

number. "Hello," she said. "Is this the Raccoon Lodge on Loon Lake?"

"Raccoons and loons?" asked Jasper. "What kind of vacation are they going on?"

Jill's mother put down the phone. "Well, that was very lucky," she said.

"Do they take pets?" Jill asked eagerly.

"They said they welcome pets," said Jill's mother.

"Fletcher, you're coming on vacation," said Jill, giving me a hug. "You'd look so cute on a snow-board."

"Who wouldn't be bored with snow?" asked Jasper. "One color: white! One temperature: cold! Why do humans go on a winter vacation? Does it mean more snow?"

"It's snow use," I warned Jasper. "I think the whole point of this vacation is the snow."

Two

The Creature in the Black Mask

It seems that getting ready for a vacation is a lot of work. Jill's mother had made Jill a list of all the things Jill had to do. Soon Jill's bedroom hardly had room for me in it. There was her brand-new snowboard in the corner. It looked like a surfboard only shorter and rounded at both ends.

Gwen was up in Jill's room going over her list. "Helmet, check!" She pointed to a bright blue helmet even bigger than a bike helmet. She checked off the big, baggy pants with suspenders, hats, gloves, boots for snowboarding, and boots for wearing after snowboarding.

"Did you know that the snowboard was invented by an eighth grader in shop class?" asked Gwen.

"That's cool," said Jill. "This is going to be the coolest vacation."

Finally the big day arrived. Gwen helped Jill and her mother pack the car. It seemed to me that they were taking half the house with them. Jill's mother brought out my dog bed and my favorite squeaky toy, a hot dog.

"In you go, Fletcher," she said. I hopped into the way-back of the car. It was a tight squeeze.

Gwen and Jill sat in the back together. "I'm so excited," said Gwen. "Jill, you and your mom will start on the bunny slope. But I checked their Web page. They've got a half-pipe, too."

"Bunnies smoking pipes?" asked Jasper. "What kind of place are we going to?"

"I don't know," I admitted. "This whole vacation thing is kind of mystifying."

A BUNNY SMOKING A PIPE.

"I'm so looking forward to relaxing," said Jill's mother.

We pulled out of the driveway. We got stuck in traffic. Jill's mother hates being caught in traffic. She looked the opposite of relaxed. "Frazzled" is the word I think would describe her.

Meanwhile in the back, I circled around three times and found a cozy position. I fell sound asleep. When I woke up, the air was crisper. I could see snowflakes falling in the headlights. It was dark when I felt the car slowing down. We pulled into a place that had Christmas lights still strung on all the trees. Christmas had been over two months ago.

The tires of the car made a crunching sound on

the driveway. Jill's mother turned off the engine.

"Listen to the silence of the country," she said.

Humans are pretty strange. There was no silence.

1) The snow was creaky and noisy as it shifted in the big snowdrifts.

2) Something was making a sharp, trilling sound—halfway between a chirp and burp.

3) I could hear the footsteps of a four-legged creature coming closer. I could smell something alive nearby. It smelled like it had recently been eating human garbage.

I got out of the car. I trotted in a circle, growling. Whatever was making that weird trilling sound was going to have to go through me to get to Jill and Gwen.

"Back off," I growled.

"You back off," screeched a high voice. "You don't have to growl at me. You're scaring me."

I peered into the darkness. Out from under a tree

came a creature wearing a black mask around its pointed snout. It had a bushy, black-ringed tail. It had long, clawed feet with five long fingers and toes.

"Why are you wearing a mask?" I asked the creature.

"It's not a mask," said the creature in a shy voice. "I'm just a raccoon . . . and I'm hungry all the time."

"You and Fletcher have a lot in common," said Jasper. "What's your name?"

"I'm Rocky Raccoon. My mother named me for a Beatles song."

"The bugs or the humans?" asked Jasper. "I just found out about the human singers, but I'm related to the bugs."

"Humans," muttered Rocky. "Most of them don't like raccoons. I don't have much use for humans either. Love their food. Hate their traps. And have you ever seen a fur coat? Scary."

"Not all humans are bad," I said. "My humans

are very nice. They feed me. They even took me on vacation."

"What's a vacation?" asked Rocky.

"It's kind of hard to explain," said Jasper.

"You're living where lots of humans come on vacation," I said to him.

"Not so many humans around here," said Rocky. "Ever since that big Mile High Ski Resort opened a few miles away, this place has been quiet. I like it that way. Most raccoons love action. I don't like action."

"You and Fletcher sound like you're related," said Jasper.

"A raccoon and a basset hound?" I said. "I don't think so."

Rocky looked a little sad.

"I don't have any relatives around here anymore," he said.

"Fletcher!" shouted Jill. "Come on."

"I'd better go before they see me," said Rocky in a scared voice. He slunk back under the tree, dragging his long, bushy tail behind him.

"He's one lonely raccoon," said Jasper.

A light went on over the front porch of the lodge. "Greetings!" shouted a cheery voice. "Welcome to Raccoon Lodge! I'm Steve Kirby! Come on in and have some hot chocolate."

Inside, there was a big fire going and a nice shaggy rug in front of the fireplace. It looked cozy.

"This must be your dog, Fletcher," said Mr. Kirby. "I'll get him some water and a dog biscuit."

I wagged my tail. I was impressed. Not only had he remembered my name, but he also had dog biscuits.

"What's he so cheery about?" whispered Jasper. Jasper wasn't in a good mood.

"He's being a good host," I said. "This is his winter resort."

Jasper looked around. "If you ask me, it looks like a place of last resort." The lights were low, but you could see that the furniture was a little shabby. I thought I smelled an animal in the corner. It smelled as musty as the furniture.

Mr. Kirby brought out a tray full of steaming hot chocolate and cookies.

As good as it smelled, I had to find out what was lurking in the corner. Black beady eyes were staring unblinking at me.

I growled.

"Oh dear," said Mr. Kirby. "I'm afraid your dog has spotted our lodge's namesake." He picked up a raccoon. Its legs were stiff. It didn't move. It looked dead. In fact, it was dead.

"We would never allow live raccoons in the house," said Mr. Kirby. "That one is stuffed. It's

been here for ages, even before I bought the lodge. I hope it didn't scare you."

"I think the only one it scared was Fletcher," teased Jill's mother.

"Well, maybe a dog biscuit will put him at ease. I just baked a batch of homemade dog biscuits," said Mr. Kirby.

I crunched it. Some dog biscuits are very dry. They taste like sawdust. But this was delicious. Crunchy, but

ME, ABOUT TO ENJOY A DOG BISCUIT.

still chewy. Still, they were a little sweet for my taste. I prefer something salty.

I heard the distant sounds of scraping on the rooftop. *SCRATCH. SCRAAATCH.*

I barked once to warn the humans.

"Shh, Fletcher," warned Jill. "You'll wake up the other guests."

"Uh . . . you don't have to worry about that," said Mr. Kirby. Before anybody could ask why, he bent down and patted my head. "Such a sweet dog," he said. "And I do believe he likes my biscuits."

Suddenly I heard the noise again. *SCRAAATCH.*

It sounded like it was coming from somewhere deep inside the house, but it was getting closer.

"You must be exhausted," said Mr. Kirby. "I'll see you to your rooms."

We walked upstairs.

SCRAAATCH! The noise was louder. "What's that sound?" asked Jill's mother. I was relieved. Finally the humans were hearing what I was hearing.

GWEN TAPPING HER BRACES

"Ah, it's nothing!" said Mr. Kirby.

"Maybe it's a ghost," said Jill.

"Or a ghoul," said Gwen, tapping her braces. She always tapped her braces when she

GHOULS ARE LEGENDARY CREATURES THAT ROB GRAVES AND EAT CORPSES.

thought a mystery was going on.

"Wouldn't that be cool?" said Jill. "We could come back and tell our friends that we met a ghoul on our winter vacation. They'd be jealous."

"They'd all want to come!" said Gwen, excitedly. "To meet the ghoul."

"Don't mind the girls, Mr. Kirby," said Jill's mother. "They're at that age where they love anything spooky. They want to go to Scotland just to see the Loch Ness Monster. I told them it's just a lake that's gotten a lot of tourists because of some silly legend."

THE LOCH NESS MONSTER IS A CREATURE SOME THINK LIVES IN LAKE NESS IN SCOTLAND. *LOCH* MEANS *LAKE* IN SCOTTISH

THUMP! Another sound on the roof showed

that the creature was coming closer. Then came more scratching.

I growled.

SCRAAAATCH!

"I don't like that sound," whispered Jasper.

Then there were two more: *THUMP! THUMP!*

"It must be a pesky raccoon," said Mr. Kirby. "I'll set up some traps."

"Maybe it's a giant raccoon who's a ghoul," said Gwen.

Jill giggled. "That would be the coolest. A giant raccoon ghoul!"

"Why does that sound cool?" asked Jasper.

A GIANT RACCOON GHOUL

"You just never know what humans want to see on vacation," I told him.

Three

Cool Ghoul Was Here

The next morning Gwen and Jill were up early. They headed downstairs for breakfast. I love the word "breakfast." It often means bacon. Everything tastes better with bacon.

"I'm so excited to try snowboarding," said Jill.

"Raccoon Lodge is built for people just starting out," said Mr. Kirby. "My bunny hill has seen lots of beginners. And even my half-pipe isn't very scary."

A HALF-PIPE

"More bunnies smoking

A BUNNY SMOKING A PIPE.

pipes," I said to Jasper. "Do you think that was the thumping noise we heard last night?"

"Where are the other guests?" asked Jill's mother.

"Uh, we're having a quiet weekend," said Mr. Kirby. Just then the door opened.

"Hi, Uncle Steve," said a young man. He had spiky hair and he was wearing baggy pants and a long jacket.

Mr. Kirby smiled, but I thought his smile was a little sad. "Oh hi, Shelby," said Mr. Kirby. "This is my nephew. He's here in case you need lessons."

"If you don't," said Shelby, "I can go to the big resort. They always need extra instructors."

"Oh, Jill and I definitely need lessons," said Jill's mother. "Gwen's done this before."

Shelby sighed.

"Now Shelby," said Mr. Kirby. "I know you'd like to get a job at the big mountain, but we have students who need you here."

"Okay, Uncle Steve," said Shelby. He turned to Jill and her mother. "First we have to find out if you are goofy footed or regular."

Jill giggled. "Fletcher's got goofy feet," she said, "but Mom and I don't."

"If you put your left foot forward naturally," explained Gwen, "that's called goofy footed."

"I always start beginners out by having them slide across Uncle's kitchen floor in socks," said Shelby. "If you put your left foot forward natu-rally, you're goofy footed. Come on into the kitchen."

I skidded across the floor. "Look!" shouted Gwen. "Fletcher's goofy footed! His left paw went first."

Shelby laughed. "I don't know if we have a

snowboard for Fletcher. But we'll get the three of you up on your boards."

Shelby opened the swinging door into the kitchen. His jaw dropped. "Uncle, what happened?"

I crawled under Shelby's leg to see what had gotten him so excited. It looked like it had snowed inside the kitchen. The floor was covered with something white, but it was not cold at all.

It got on my nose. I licked it. It was flour. And best of all, it tasted like salami.

"It's the flour I use to make my biscuits!" shouted Mr. Kirby. He pointed to the corner. "And look: There's a chewed-up salami. That raccoon must have gotten in through the pet door again."

"This wasn't an ordinary raccoon," yelled Jill. She pointed to the middle of the floor. The words COOL GHOUL! were written in animal tracks in the flour. It looked as if it had been done by a creature who had long front and hind paws.

CHEWED SALAMI

CLOSE-UP OF A RACCOON PAW PRINT ⟶

"Those are raccoon tracks!" said Mr. Kirby.

"No ordinary raccoon could have written that!" said Shelby.

Gwen stared at me. She tapped her braces. "I know one creature who loves salami more than anything," she said. "Fletcher."

Jill held up one of my paws. "His paws don't look like that. And besides, dogs can't read. And they certainly can't write."

"Raccoons are smart animals," said Shelby.

"Not that smart," said Mr. Kirby, "unless we have a raccoon with supernatural powers."

"Do you think you really have a cool ghoul who's a raccoon?" asked Jill.

"Well, I wouldn't want to spread rumors," said Mr. Kirby. "We *have* had a little trouble with raccoons lately. Even the brand-new lodge has raccoons. But nothing like this."

Jill's mother had her video camera out. "I'll get some pictures of this. If a raccoon is getting into the house, you should probably call the exterminator about it."

"Exterminator!" shrieked Jasper. "That's all we need. What kind of a vacation is this?"

"Mom," said Jill, "raccoons are cute. They shouldn't be exterminated."

"These exterminators just trap them and take them far away so they won't come back," said Shelby.

"An exterminator would be useless if it's a ghoul," said Gwen, tapping her braces.

"Don't let your imaginations run away with you," warned Jill's mother.

"I hate to think about Rocky the shy raccoon in a trap," whispered Jasper. "He's afraid of traps."

Four
Destructive Little Creature

"We've got to find Rocky!" I said to Jasper as the humans got ready to snowboard. "We'll go out the pet door. It's probably the way he came in."

Jasper shivered. "It's cold outside. There are piles of fresh snow bigger than you."

"We have to warn him," I said.

"Give me a minute," said Jasper. He burrowed into my coat and pulled out some loose fur. Within minutes he had knit himself a hat and mittens.

"Okay," he said. "I'm ready."

JASPER KNITTING
FLETCHER'S FUR

We went out the pet door. The cold winter air felt tingly but very clean. The sun lit the snow. Dark pools of forest stood out on the hills.

I tried to see if I could smell a raccoon. They have a distinctive odor, and I have a very good sniffer.

I went into the woods a little way. The odor of a live raccoon was getting stronger. The smell was coming from a pile of dead leaves in a hollow tree stump.

"Rocky!" I barked. "We've got to talk to you. You're in trouble!"

I stuck my nose into the hollow of the log. Rocky was sleeping in a ball, his long black ringed tail curled around him to keep him warm.

"Get up!" I pushed him with my nose.

Rocky rubbed his eyes with his almost human-like front paws.

"What?" he asked. "Why are you waking me up?"

"It's daytime," said Jasper. "You should be up."

"We raccoons are nocturnal animals," said Rocky. "That means that we are most active at night."

"Well, we saw what you did last night," Jasper yelled. "Why did you write 'Cool Ghoul' in flour in the kitchen? The words looked like they were written in raccoon tracks!"

"I didn't do it!" squeaked Rocky.

"Could it have been one of your relatives?" I asked Rocky.

"All my relatives moved over to the big resort. The garbage is much better over there."

"Well, Mr. Kirby is calling the exterminator," I told him. "You're being blamed."

"Do you know what exterminators do?" sobbed Rocky. "Even when they think they're being humane, they trap us and take us far, far away from any place we've ever known. They never want us to come back. This is my home! I don't want to leave!" Rocky started to wail.

"Stop weeping," I said. A weeping raccoon is a very sad sight. Rocky was crying so hard he could hardly hear me.

"Get a grip!" I barked at him. I must have said it a little louder than I expected.

"Fletcher?" shouted Jill from on top of the hill. "Hey, Gwen, Fletcher's outside! Come, Fletcher!"

I turned around.

"Oh no," yelped Rocky. "Your humans will tell the exterminator where to find me."

"Not my humans," I tried to tell him. Rocky scampered up a tree and out of sight.

"Hey, Fletcher! Over here," shouted Gwen. "Come watch!"

I could see Gwen and Jill's bright green and blue helmets up on the hill. Then Jill fell down on her butt. Gwen kept her feet on the board. She was riding the hill as if it were a giant wave.

Gwen skidded to a stop right in front of me.

Jill got back up for a moment, and then fell again, sliding down the gentle slope on her butt. "This is harder than it looks," she said as she landed near me.

"You're getting it," said Shelby, swooping down near her. "Just keep your legs bent. You want to look like a boxer: ready for anything."

"A boxer?" asked Jasper. "Who would want to see a human girl look like a big dog like a boxer?"

"I think he means the athlete, not the dog," I said to Jasper.

"Shelby!" shouted Gwen. "Can I try the half-pipe? I've done it before." Gwen pointed to the part of the hill that looked like a half circular pile of snow with the edges going way up to the sky.

"Well," said Shelby. "I don't think Jill and her mother are quite ready for that yet. But if you take it slowly, you and I can try to show them how it's done."

"Come on, Fletcher!" said Jill. "You can ride the chairlift in my lap. Don't you want to see Gwen show us her stuff?"

"Tell them no," whispered Jasper, shivering. "I don't want to go on any chair that's lifting. It looks cold up there."

"Gwen really wants us to watch her," I said to Jasper. "Besides, Rocky went up a tree. Maybe I'll see him from up on top of the hill."

I climbed onto Jill's lap. The chairlift was kind of fun. My ears flapped in the breeze.

When we got to the top, Shelby took off first. He hopped once to turn the board downhill and then he was off. He quickly shifted directions and the board curved in the air. As he turned he was drawing long graceful curving lines behind him, like brush strokes on a canvas. You could tell he was an expert.

Gwen took off. Because she was lighter than Shelby, she seemed to fly through the air even faster. She hit a small jump to one side of the trail and her board went up into the air, and bounced into a landing.

She went up the other side of the half-pipe, flying through the air. Suddenly she let out a scream. She went over the lip of the half-pipe.

"Oh no!" screamed Jill. Jill and her mother tried slip-sliding down the hill at the same time that Shelby was climbing back up.

"Gwen! Are you all right?" yelled Shelby.

"I'm fine!" shouted Gwen. "But look!"

COOL GHOUL IS HERE! was written in the snow.

The letters were spelled out in raccoon tracks just like in the kitchen.

"I don't believe it!" said Jill's mother, taking out her camera. "Somebody should get Mr. Kirby. This is very strange."

Just then Mr. Kirby came chugging up the hill in a Sno-Cat. A man dressed in a red-and-black hunting jacket was with him. I wondered if that was the exterminator.

"Uncle Steve!" shouted Shelby. "Did you know about this?"

"Know about what?" asked Mr. Kirby. "I was just coming up with the local newspaper's reporter. He got a tip about what happened in our kitchen. I told him that our guest took some pictures."

"Your cool ghoul struck again!" shouted Jill. "Gwen took a tumble when she saw it." Gwen and Jill pointed to the letters in the snow.

"Oh my!" said Mr. Kirby. The reporter jumped out and started snapping pictures.

"This is something!" said the reporter. "We got an anonymous phone call at the paper about the writing in the kitchen. Who was the first one to spot this new writing in the snow?"

"I was," said Gwen. "I was catching air off my jump. I looked down and there it was!"

"Well, I never knew of a raccoon that could write!" said the reporter. "Usually raccoons are such destructive little creatures."

I heard a sharp gasping little trill. I looked up in a tree. I saw black eyes surrounded by patches of black fur, and a little pair of white-rimmed ears.

It was Rocky. The destructive little creature looked scared to death.

Five

Hullabaloo

The next day the local newspaper had a front-page article about the Cool Ghoul at Raccoon Lodge.

Jill's mother read the article out loud at breakfast. "'The Raccoon Lodge, known for its quiet, has had quite a hullabaloo this week. Could there really be a ghoul that likes to disguise itself as a raccoon? The owner, Steven Kirby, laughs but admits that he has no way to explain how twice in one day, raccoon tracks spelled out the words "Cool Ghoul!" With his own eyes this reporter saw the lettering spelled out in the snow. One of the young guests was so excited that she couldn't stop tapping her braces. . . .'"

"He means you, Gwen," said Jill.

Jill's mother laughed. "Well, we certainly arrived in the middle of a hullabaloo."

"I wonder what will happen today!" said Gwen.

Mr. Kirby came bustling in.

"Did you see the newspaper?" he asked. "We're the talk of the town. I've already got a dozen new reservations of people wanting to come up for the chance that they'll get a sighting of the cool ghoul."

"But have you called the exterminator?" asked Jill's mother.

"I wish she would stop asking about that," said Jasper.

"You know, the exterminator slipped my mind with all the excitement," admitted Mr. Kirby. "I'll call him now."

Mr. Kirby went to the telephone.

"We've got to find Rocky again," I said to Jasper. "This time the exterminator is really coming."

I snuck out the pet door and went back to Rocky's den where I had found him sleeping before.

But the den was empty.

"Rocky!" I barked.

I heard a high pitched trilling sound, like someone moaning, high on the hill.

I looked up. There was Rocky waving his little paws to me. He was at the top of the snowboarding half-pipe.

I bounded up the side of the hill and then I skidded to a stop.

"You've got to hide," I told him. "They're really calling the exterminator this time."

"How can I hide?" said Rocky. "Look!" He pointed his little clawed paw down the slope.

It wasn't just raccoon tracks anymore. Huge

letters were carved in snow along the slope: COOL GHOUL.

Surrounding each letter were raccoon tracks, hundreds of raccoon tracks.

"You couldn't have done this," I said to Rocky.

"Of course I didn't," wailed Rocky. "Even if I stayed up all night, I couldn't have done it. But look at the tracks. They look like my footprints! Who is going to believe me?" Rocky was so excited that he was walking around in circles. I studied his tracks.

"Wait a minute!" I said. "Your tracks sink into the snow. But the tracks around the letters—they don't. Those tracks are just on top of the snow as if the cool ghoul didn't weigh anything."

"How is that going to help me?" whined Rocky.

"I don't think it's a ghoul!" I said. "Remember Shelby said that he wished he could teach at the big resort. Maybe he did this so Raccoon Lodge

would close down. He could have used the stuffed raccoon to make the tracks."

"Even if that's true," wailed Rocky. "Who will believe you? Even you can't talk to humans and make them understand that it wasn't me."

"I've got two wonderful humans who might be able to help," I said. "Stay here."

I bounded back down through the snow to where Gwen and Jill were just putting on their snowboards.

I barked.

"You'd better take Fletcher inside," said Shelby. "You don't want him disturbing the other snowboarders. Yesterday the slope was empty. But today we're going to have a crowd. Everyone wants to see if the cool ghoul has come back."

If I was right and Shelby was the culprit, then his little plan had backfired. More people than ever were coming to his uncle's resort. I barked again and pulled on Jill's mittened hand.

"Fletcher wants us to go with him," said Gwen. "He wouldn't be making such a fuss if it weren't important."

Gwen and Jill followed me, and so did Jill's mother and Shelby.

Rocky was hiding up in a tree.

"Look!" shouted Jill as she noticed the huge letters sculpted out of snow. "The Cool Ghoul has struck again."

My paws sunk into the snow. "Whoof!" I said, sticking my nose into my paw print.

Gwen began to tap her braces. "Hey, wait a minute," she said. "Look at Fletcher's paw prints."

I nodded and pointed my nose at the raccoon tracks, lifting my goofy left paw like a hunting dog.

"The raccoon tracks don't sink into the snow,"

said Gwen, tapping her braces with her mittened hand.

"That's because it's a ghoul," said Jill.

I sighed. I knew it wasn't a ghoul or a raccoon. There was just one species who would have done this: a human. But how could I prove it?

Just then a man came charging up the hill with a big steel metal trap.

"The exterminator," said Jasper in a terrified voice.

"Hey!" shouted Jill's mother. "There's the raccoon." She dropped her snowboard and pointed up to the tree, where poor Rocky's big ringed tail was hanging down.

"Fletcher!" whispered Rocky. "Help me. I don't want to go into a trap."

"You've got to save him," whispered Jasper.

I jumped onto the back of the snowboard. "Come on, Rocky!" I shouted. Rocky jumped on the front.

We went sailing down the half-pipe!

We carved turns around the letters that spelled out "Cool Ghoul!"

"I'm flying!" shouted Jasper. "I'm a flea who flies with Fletcher!"

We skidded to a stop right at the back of the lodge. Mr. Kirby was out in the snow. When he saw me, his mouth flew open, and his hand opened wide. That's when I saw it!

In his hand, he had the stuffed raccoon. And the letters COO were already spelled out in raccoon tracks.

"Oh dear!" shouted Mr. Kirby. He tried to bury the stuffed raccoon in the snow before the others could find us.

I barked. It wasn't Shelby who wanted to keep people away from the Raccoon Lodge. It was Mr. Kirby. And he was doing it so that the lodge would

become famous! But how would I tell the humans?

Gwen and Jill came roaring down the hill, quickly followed by Shelby and Jill's mother.

"Fletcher, that was awesome!" shouted Jill. She put her arms around me.

"I got it all on video!" said Jill's mother.

Rocky hid in a snowbank with just his little snout sticking out.

The exterminator came barreling down the hill. "I think I see the raccoon," he said.

I dug into the snow and pulled out the stuffed raccoon. I dropped it at Gwen and Jill's feet right near the letters COO.

"This raccoon is already dead," said the exterminator, sounding a little disappointed. "It's stuffed."

Gwen stared at Mr. Kirby. "You were starting to spell out the letters using the stuffed raccoon. There never was a Cool Ghoul," she accused.

ROCKY'S NOSE

THE EXTERMINATOR

Mr. Kirby hung his head in shame. "You were the ones who gave me the idea. I've been losing customers to the big new resort, but I thought if the lodge became famous for something like the Cool Ghoul people would come. But now that you know the truth, I may have to close the lodge."

"I bet people would come to a place where pets are welcome and you and Shelby can try to teach the pets to snowboard," said Jill. "There's no place in the world like that."

"Gwen's right," said Shelby. "It might be fun to teach pets."

"I've got it all on video," said Jill's mother. "I bet lots of people would love to see that video. You could use it in an ad."

"They'll all want to come to see the place where it was made," said Jill's mother. "Especially when we tell them that the food's delicious too."

"You can tell them that you're the home of the original Snowboard-Riding Basset Hound and His Raccoon Companion," said Jill.

"Is that me they're talking about?" whispered Rocky from his snowbank.

"It is," I told him. "You're famous!"

"Not as famous as you are!" said Jasper.

"Come on, Fletcher," said Gwen. "Do you want to do it again?"

I shook my head. Once was exciting. But twice would be foolhardy.

"Maybe I should try to whip him up some fresh dog biscuits," said Mr. Kirby.

I wagged my tail. Now all I had to do was to find a way for him to put a little salami into those dog biscuits.

Then he'd really be famous.